LORETTA WELCH

Yankee Doodle

After studying in Trinity College, Dublin, and working in publishing in San Francisco, Loretta Welch landed in Boston's North End, steps away from the shore on which her immigrant ancestors first set foot, five generations ago. *Yankee Doodle* is Welch's first book.

Open Door

First published by GemmaMedia in 2011.

GemmaMedia
230 Commercial Street
Boston, MA 02109 USA

www.gemmamedia.com

Printed in the United States of America

15 14 4 5

978-1-934848-53-1

Library of Congress Cataloging-in-Publication Data

Welch, Loretta, 1955-
Yankee Doodle / Loretta Welch.
p. cm. -- (Gemma open door)
ISBN 978-1-934848-53-1
1. Boston (Mass.)--Fiction. 2. Immigrants--Fiction. I. Title.
PS3623.E46235Y36 2011
813'.6--dc22
2010045821

Cover by Night & Day Design

Inspired by the Irish series of books designed for adult literacy, Gemma Open Door Foundation provides fresh stories, new ideas and resources for young people and adults as they embrace the power of reading and the written word.

For Kathleen

CONTENTS

INTRODUCTION

Memory

"Oh my god, oh my god, ohmy-god!"

"He is, like, the weirdest teacher, and he actually, like, made a joke!"

"English is, like, so dull and then he goes, he goes, he goes . . . "

"'Class bewitched!'" squawked the shortest.

" . . . and I looked at Hai and we were like, ohmygod!"

The brace of teenagers burst on to the car, a second or two before the doors closed. Three flew into seats, and the others grabbed at holding rails, looking like they were about to do chin-ups over their lucky friends, or maybe drool on their heads. iPod cords and other wires dangled like ornaments on jeans, back-packs, and out of a couple of ears.

"I thought maybe he came from, I don't know, like Idaho or Duluth or something. So lame." These kids talked fast, really fast.

"Those shoes, man. I'm, like, my GRANDdad wouldn't wear them."

"Yeah, but you can hear him coming, Thuy. Handy on Fridays!"

"More like Mars. Landed in the corn and became, like, a zombie."

"You see Lien's neck? She says the Revere Vampire's still 'at large.' " Fingers making quotation marks.

"Bet it was Bao. They hit the mall

during world history. Some vampire. So gross."

"And then, did you die? At lunch, Minh was telling Sean, and he, like, laughed so hard milk came out of his nose."

"So weird, I never drink milk at my house."

"Me neither . . . get off! . . . but I always drink it at school."

"So we were, like, 'whatever.' Central Square is always, like, SO FULL. Oh wait, there's room up there. Run!"

And the whole group squealed and lurched to the end of the car and kept up the review of their school day. The skinny boy with a pink streak on the very peak of his hair landed almost on top of Stella. She had been watching and dodged the backpack . . . just.

"So, Mr Kavanagh is like, sort of, funny!"

"Oh, come ON! He's human. Well, sort of. I'm sure he, like, just made a mistake."

Coming home on the Red Line, as the train came out of the ground and up over the Charles River, Stella leaned her head back against the ad for night school and closed her eyes. She felt the late afternoon sun flicker over her face as the car passed the towers on what locals call the Salt and Pepper Bridge. She was tired, and it felt good to rest and let the light play on her eyelids. Rocking back and forth with the motion, she got a little closer to sleep and remembered another time, another overheard conversation, another trip on this train. She smiled.

ONE

Stella Comes To Town

From Ashmont to Mattapan, the subway changes to an old trolley car, the kind they built when the oldest underground railway in the country was brand new. Like a brave little toy train, a single car picks up riders who get out of the "real" train, and then it takes them to their final stop. Passing the back yards and shuttered windows of houses lining the track, people look out on triple-deckers and an old mill over the river that used to bring power to a brick factory along its banks. Left empty long ago, the plant is hung with signs offering fixed-up lofts for sale to young people looking for new homes. The trolley car passes by an antique cemetery, so old nobody can be buried there anymore. The glass in the train windows is aged, and a good bit dirty, and it casts the view outside in sepia, that yellow tint that makes movies look old.

Stella took her place each day between the mothers with strollers and the tall kids with big sneakers, always untied. Many kinds of people joined her, leaving their houses to get to someplace else: maybe work, maybe school, maybe family in another part of town. Wherever they were going, the riders on this little train woke and opened their eyes as the train took them closer to their destination and farther from home.

Home. That was a funny word for

Stella. She wasn't born here, but out in the vast, flat Midwest. Her dad moved the family around quite a bit, looking for work. Labor, mostly. They called hard work *labor*, and her dad was good at hard work. Work for hard men. But he had the habit of quick anger followed by fast punches, and that often meant jobs didn't last too long. Still, although she had lived in many cities and towns, there was something the same about places in the middle of the country. Just as there was something very different about this city in the east. Boston. Sometimes she pinched the inside of her arm to remind herself she really did live here.

Comparing the two places, she often thought about her childhood. She remembered a lot of things, some good and some bad, but all were parts of her. That she knew for certain, just as she felt this new home would make a mark on her, too.

If she had one favorite memory, it was that big old tree with the hammock hung from its lowest branches on one side and the shed roof on the other. It was Cindy's house, and they were fourteen. Cindy's mom was pretty casual about what they did at nighttime, so they slept out in the hammock, swinging in the dark shadow of the sweet tree. They could hear the clatter of the nightly trains coming a good mile away before they would roar past Cindy's lawn, not two blocks from the siding. For hours, they talked about moving away as the summer stars spun in the sky above them. Stella supposed she was happiest there, comparing notes on the kids that were rotten to them in school, smelling the warm breeze as it washed over the cornfield and planning grown-up lives in the Big City—Minneapolis or maybe Chicago.

Then her dad lit out for yet another new job, in Kansas, promising to send for Stella and her mom when he was settled. "Might as well go and stay with your cousin, Gerty. Save a little for the trip." She had said a fast goodbye to Cindy after algebra and made her promise to remember. That was the last she saw of her father, and it took her a year to miss him.

"I'm pretty new here," she would say to people who asked her questions or wanted directions. "Just getting my sea legs." She thought she was funny and sounded like a sailor. The ocean startled her. She had seen huge fields of wheat and corn in Illinois and Iowa, and sometimes they seemed endless. On the hottest summer days, with the sun burning in the middle of the sky, the open spaces were almost too much to bear.

But nothing prepared her for how wide and how deep the sea was, spread in front of her. She thought of those old-fashioned people who came from places far away over that ocean to the New World. She expected some were happy, excited by the trip, and some were just plain scared. On rainy days, she thought of the ships that crashed against the rocks before they made it to America and wondered whether anybody knew the names of their passengers. When she could, she took the T to Wonderland to walk the beach at Revere. She loved spotting the sea between buildings on the Red Line between UMass Boston and Andrew Station.

She looked at boats in the harbor and imagined how far each one could go. The small boats could get you to Cape Cod, where tourists ate lobster and wore bright green pants with whales on them. Bigger ships, the ones with puffy sails, could get you as far as Maine, maybe even Canada, as long as you stayed close to the shore. It was the big ships that docked in South Boston that could go far. Braver than all of them, they could turn away from the land and head right out onto the ocean, straight across that deep blue sea with never a look back at the shore for days on end. Those were ships, Stella nodded. Still, a little boat with two small sails could take a girl to coves and sandy beaches, and that would be just fine with her. There are lots of ways to get people where they are going, she reckoned, and many places to end up, too.

When she first came east, she thought about "home" a lot.

TWO

Red Line, Or Stella Goes To Work

The Red Line travels up from the south of the city along the shore and into downtown Boston. It stops at South Station where passengers mix with commuters coming in from the suburbs, heading to their jobs in the big banks and high-storied buildings. Park Street, the historical and tourist center of the town, is the next stop. Here you find government offices and more banks. Every quarter hour, the old church bells sing out over the park below, Stella's favorite spot. Then the train heads to Mass General, up out of the ground and above the river, crossing into Cambridge over the

Longfellow Bridge. Riders spot the sailing clubs beneath the science museum, as students sail up the Charles and along the lip of the Back Bay. Beacon Hill snuggles close to the sky in back.

The Red Line goes for miles and miles, over land and through tunnels, under the brains of MIT, the cultural mix of Central Square, and the tony blocks of Harvard. Then it goes downmarket to upcoming Porter Square and the hope of urban middle classes. Finally it heads out past Somerville and its pasty statues to Alewife, known for commuter parking, the backside of Fresh Pond and the high-rise apartments that remind Stella of grain silos. And though she took the Red Line just about every day to one cleaning job or another, on trains as full as cattle cars, she swore she never saw the same person twice. Not once.

As Stella made her progress each day, she grew brave enough to look into the faces of her fellow riders. Once, she found herself looking into a sweet face that reminded her of her mother when she was older. Some of the ladies she cleaned for reminded her of her mother, too. There was a smell in their apartments, a little bit of hairspray, something a little sweet and something a little sour, like laundry.

She still missed her mom, and it made her sad to see her slippers, tucked into her suitcase all those years ago when she left Kansas. There was something in the way her mother tipped her head and a comical pitch to her laugh, although she couldn't really remember the sound any more. Come to think of it, she couldn't remember much. But the lady in the birdbath hat across from her drew her in. Stella started to smile and then remembered to avoid eye contact. Eye contact was supposed to be rude. Or dangerous. Or both. In any case, she turned away and stared out of the window that threw her own reflection back at her in the tunnel. She saw her mom's face in her own, and watched the mirrored lady fall asleep.

Stella discovered so very many mysteries on the Red Line.

She wondered if anybody else thought that putting kids on those leashes mothers use makes them look like pets. A baby-faced boy with a suitcase got off for the Silver Line, and she couldn't understand how someone that young could possibly be wearing a wedding ring. More and more people looked younger to her these days, as though grown-up jobs and adult lives were being handed to children fresh out of school, and she was still stuck in homeroom.

And what about all those wires and earpieces people wear? How many people could be listening to the same thing? The man who turned his cap from front to back and back to front twice going under South Station was a puzzle. Was it a mile marker? For good luck?

Hats, now there was a curiosity. Peaked, floppy, feathered, veiled. Beanies, berets, bowlers and fedoras of all colors, on men and on women. She didn't see as many cowboy hats as she grew up with, but they were fairly well represented, all right. Of course, every variety of baseball cap under the sun was worn in every which way. Stella figured there was some code, but she couldn't make it out. Young, fierce, red-faced men curled their visors until they were almost tubes sticking out from the middles of their heads. An especially round Yankees fan looked so squeezed into his hat that rhinos came to mind.

She got used to seeing caps, front to back or back to front, on top of snow hats, which looked goofy to her, but it got funnier. Out past Porter Square, in the middle of winter, the man down the car sported a knit hat, a scarf, a baseball cap (she recognized the Cubs; where did he get that?) earmuffs and a floppy thing like you'd wear in the jungle. In that order. She couldn't make out his face, but figured he was from someplace very far away and a whole lot warmer.

A baby's eyes peered out of her chubby face, swallowed in a pink hat, at a young man with his head hidden in a parka hood. At the end of the day, the subway was peppered with caps and scarves and single gloves left behind. A tiny blue mitten lay on the seat, long separated from its little boy. Did they miss them when they were home? Is there a Lost and Found for abandoned pork pies?

Mysteries. Most of all, she wanted to know where they all came from, these fellow riders, these commuters, these travelers in a tube underground. She knew there were Haitians and Russians and people from Vermont. There were people on vacation, going to a game, going to walk the Freedom Trail, working in a shop, selling from a case, watching for a theft. All kinds of people riding the subway looked perfectly at home, well, at least like they belonged there. And all the time she felt like there was a great big sign over her head that said "misfit."

Whole communities sprang up in the subway and then drifted apart. The crush of people between three in the afternoon and six in the evening, especially in the downtown switching stations, had an energy all their own. They were eager to get home, taking off coats, putting on earphones, huddling next to the yellow lines that kept you at a safe distance from the train. *Did they see me?*

When Stella rode the subway, she thought about these mysteries a lot.

THREE

Neighbors

"You have to stop working so much, Stella, and don't be riding that train so late!"

Mrs Washington was always giving out about Stella's hours, but mostly she just liked to talk to the girl. It took her three months to start when Stella moved into the building. Mrs W was leery of a girl from out of town with little luggage and no furniture. But one day, Stella let the cable guy in for her, and Mrs W warmed up. She was due to go to the foot doctor, and "hell or high water" she was going to make that appointment. Mrs W dearly loved her sports channels, though, so her conflict was profound when the cable company gave her Tuesday, 8 am to 1 pm; be there or forget about the playoffs. Stella watched over the installation and signed her own name to the forms. Mrs W definitely warmed up.

They never, ever stepped into each other's apartments, except that rare day when the television made them friends. Mrs W chatted to Stella on the stoop or in the hall on subjects ranging from the weather ("passable" or "dreadful") to the Red Sox ("mostly break your heart") to landlords ("all money and no soul") to today's news ("good thing Mr W is not here to see this") to her grandson ("love that boy, but he's a fool").

Mrs W got the short version of Stella's arrival in Boston, Stella seeing no reason for darker details. What passed for her story: parents gone ("enough said") and taken in by an aunt ("bless her heart"). One topic that always brought out the protector in Mrs W was Stella's plan for night courses when she could raise enough money to pay the fees. Mrs W couldn't imagine it would take that long to get a degree and find a job as a medical assistant or an x-ray technician or a whatever and "bug on out of here," as Stella teased. Secretly, Mrs W hoped it would take longer.

"Statistics? You study statistics? What in the world would statistics have to do with a busted arm? I swear they make things up to charge people for learning. I was a girl, numbers were done in your head. None of this calculator business. In your head. My grandson couldn't recite the multiplication tables on a bet.

"But you have a head for it, Stella. I can tell just looking at you."

And Stella? She just didn't talk much. Her mother said the cat had got her tongue. But then her father had said, just wait 'til she starts, they won't be able to put a lid on her.

When she first moved east, Stella went months without talking to anyone outside of her aunt, and that was brief. Stella had heard so many stories about how cold people were in places like Boston and New York that she was terrified to open her mouth, lest someone, who knew, yelled at her or threw something at her head. And it was a little true, Mrs W had to admit; people could be downright rude when they were in a hurry to get here or there. "But people are good, if you give them a chance, and it wouldn't hurt to talk to the postman once in a while, for goodness sake." Stella now made it a point to comment on the weather to every clerk in the corner store.

"Statistics can be interesting, to a point," Stella said.

"Point is right. The point of all that study is to make something of yourself, and here you are, a long, long way from home and studying up with those people who have more money than sense. Making something of yourself. Even though you're not from here, and it's hard if you're not from here, there you go. Just like you were born to have it. Good lord, girl, it must be hard for you."

"I have hope, Mrs W."

"And so you should, Stella. So you should."

FOUR

Mrs F

Mrs F lived on the fifth floor, and Stella had to get buzzed in every time. It was a pain with the buckets and the mops, but Mrs F had her own vacuum to use, insisted on it. It made the train ride less of a hassle every third Wednesday, she reckoned.

Stella liked everything about the place, the lace curtains and the shiny furniture. "Mahogany wood, Stella, and you aren't allowed buy it anymore. It's illegal like jade and whale teeth."

Stella didn't mind the knickknacks that had to be moved, one by one, or the doilies that had to be ironed every other month. Not even dusting the walls with a rag wrapped around a broom bothered her, but really, who dusts the walls? She liked that everything was tiny and in its place. Salt and pepper shakers were shaped like little lamps, tiny dogs, mushrooms. Some were very small flowerpots, and they matched. Matching things was not something to worry about when Stella grew up.

The only thing that got her peeved happened in the last ten minutes, when Stella had pushed the couch back in place and fluffed up the pillows, checked the statues on the TV to make sure they were in exactly the right spot and stood waiting by the door with her buckets and her purse.

"Now, are you sure you swept under

the bed? I won't have the dust we had last time."

"Yes, ma'am."

"And what about the garbage pail? If there is an odor, every cat in the neighborhood will be scratching at my door, and I can't stand cats."

"It's clean, Mrs F."

"Well now, what if I pay you next time for two?"

And Stella looked down, rubbing her toe into the mat at the door, saying as loud as she could "Bad idea," without actually saying it. You could never get two payments out of Mrs F. She wouldn't believe you.

"Oh, well, wait a minute. Let me just think if I have any cash today. Things are so dear."

"Why do you put up with that woman?" Mrs W would ask. Stella made the mistake of telling her about Mrs F's short memory when it came to owed wages, and Mrs W never tired of scolding her.

Stella rode the T to Mrs F from early spring throughout the summer and late into fall. She watched the colors change in the trees along the river as the train came up over the bridge. Toward the end of November, all the leaves were off the trees, and the river took on a dusty grey color. Mrs F looked a little grey, too.

Stella started to move more pill jars than knickknacks. Boxes of tissue piled up in every room. There was something gone funny with her joints, Mrs F reported, and her breathing was hard.

Stella started to notice other things,

too. The pantry, for example, which was really just a small cupboard between the kitchen and the living room. More medicine bottles filled the shelves, easing out the sugar and the teabags and the three kinds of store cookies Mrs F always had "for company." Along about the first of January, the bottles got fewer, but the shelves never filled up again. Stella saw the cans of tuna, half empty in the icebox.

"Will you make sure the bedspread is straight like I like it, dear? And don't rush off so. I'll need to see, do I have any cash today. That market would rob you blind."

Mrs F lifted her frail little body from the chair and shuffled into her bedroom. She opened the top drawer of a dresser that must have been hers as a bride. Usually, Stella was left behind a closed door when the old woman fished for her pocketbook. Of late, security was lax.

"It's okay, Mrs F. You paid two weeks last time."

Very quietly, Mrs F said, "Why yes, child, I did," and watched Stella unlatch the door.

FIVE

Red Line, Or Stella Hears Music

There seemed to be plenty of ways to make money, even underground.

The worst job had to be the newsstand under Government Center, because you had to go two whole flights below ground level. It's creepy to hear heavy trains rattling over your head, Stella thought, and wondered how the guy deals with the noise. People working the Park Street shop, on the other hand, could almost see the open sky at the top of the stairs.

A lot of time, waiting on all those trains, they had entertainment. Stella was at first shocked and then thrilled to see so many people making music in the stations, collecting money for their talent with an open case or a little bucket. Some had posters, some sold CDs. Some just played their hearts out. She loved the old man with the violin who worked the Blue Line, although she worried the air wasn't too good for him. And she always dropped a coin in the open accordion case before Blonde Bob, as she called him, a tall, lanky Texan, or so he said, who "came to charm y'all out of yer hard-earned with a little somethin' I wrotes."

The most famous stop was Harvard Square, and once or twice, Stella got out on her way home. She wandered around the brick buildings and the chain stores, trying to figure out who the brainy students were, but they all looked like adults in kids' bodies, with big handbags and smart phones. She wasn't sure what to look at so she walked into a bookstore, and, boy, was she surprised; comics were weird these days. Could you really call them books at all? If they were, she would have done great had she stayed in school. She thought about coffee, but the shops were too full and too expensive. A simple cup of joe cost three bucks. She watched the chess games in the middle of the crowd for a while, but since she didn't know the rules, she didn't know who was winning. Still, it gave her a place to stand for ten minutes and not keep moving, moving, moving.

Down past the center of the square, on a winding street, she saw street performers in the entrances to shops. They reminded her of the church fair booths, one to a storefront, and she marveled that anybody had the nerve to stand out in the street and sing or dance or juggle or ride or do magic. The bad ones she felt sorry for, but the really good ones scared her half to death, drawing bystanders in as though they had some secret magnet or powerful spell. Stella wrapped her arms around her bag and looked at these performers and bet they would all be famous someday. She pretended she was fishing for coins in her pocket and looked surprised when her hand came out empty. Stella moved along.

One night, going home a little later than she would have liked, she saw a young couple who looked like they were from another time. They were on the middle platform in Park Street, and Stella had gotten out of the car she was riding when a group of very loud sports fans coming from a ball game got too close. She stepped out and waited for the next train, and then she waited for another.

The boy was red-haired, wore jeans and a suit jacket and sported a weathered guitar. "Martin," it said on the neck. He had twinkly eyes and a charming mouth that made him look older than his age, which couldn't have been twenty. He sounded old-fashioned, Old World, maybe Irish or English, and called himself a busker. When he sang, Stella thought she was listening to a recording, his voice was so round and so sweet.

Beside him stood a dark-haired girl, curly waves down to her shoulder, bangles up to her elbow, in a set of clothes that almost looked like a costume. Willowy, long skirt and dark blouse that made a *v* below her neck. The whole effect was like a studio picture, like the ones Stella's pals had made when they graduated high school, the ones that made girls look like cameo rings. Stella could not tell if she was foreign, too, but she thought not. You could barely hear her as she tried to harmonize with her big fellow.

Nor could Stella work out if she was happy or not. She had that soft look in her downcast eyes that came either from being a young woman in love or a scared girl in a big city. Whatever it was, these two were clearly performing for keeps. They were light-hearted and serious all at the same time; they needed the money, but beyond that, they needed each other. And for the first time, Stella thought she might have seen someone, like herself, who did not quite fit into the picture. She let a few go by, and when she finally boarded a train for home, she saw the red-haired boy put his hand out to help his young lady climb the stairs.

SIX

Lost

There was a spot in the middle of her back, more up than down, between her shoulders, that felt like it was going to break. She knew it wasn't possible, because there were no bones there, but when she put her bags down and picked them back up again as the train arrived, tears came to her eyes. She had to stand against a wall sometimes to straighten up. Her posture wasn't great, and the weight of all those supplies, all that dust swept up, and a million swipes back and forth across window panes made her ache. When the sky was blue and the birds sang at her in the evening, when it was summertime and the wind was warm, it went away when she looked up. Stella wondered how much of the ache was an old unhappiness.

Not unhappiness, really, just that steady gnawing feeling that she didn't belong. The trouble was, where she came from didn't seem too cozy, either. Where was this girl supposed to be? Certain days, she figured somebody would pluck her up out of the line of people waiting at open doors and cast her back into a pool of people. Or whisk her up in the air on a dust cloud, far far away where she didn't stand out, but where was that?

From the Midwest, where she was "drug up," she brought phrases like "old as dirt," and "dark as four-forty-five," but she never said "warsh" for "wash" or "growed up" for "grown up." And while she knew exactly what someone meant when they said "she ain't never came," her diction was almost without a place. Like her. She mixed up some words, for sure. "Missouri" was "Missouruh," and "soda" was "pop." But it sure as heck wasn't "tonic." Still, she got used to the locals who took *r*'s out of words like "pahk" and "gahden" and dropped them at random into other words like "idear." She worked out that Mrs F's "hassock" was a footstool, but these "rotaries" for cars were just plain chaos, as far as she was concerned. Try to cross one in the middle of the day.

How people talk, their language, has something to do with belonging, too. Everything from a foreign language to the inside chatter of teenagers made you a part of a group. Or a place. Or a family. And Stella felt those were all gone for her. And then she thought: These are things that made you who you are, so you take them with you anyway. Maybe you belong where you are. She just wasn't tethered any more, like a boat without a sail. So much was lost.

Stella knew loss was something like hurt, only deeper. Once in a while a storm comes up behind your eyes and tears can form. Most of the time, it's like a bellyache, a little higher, and when it comes, it seeps into the rest of your muscles. Simple sadness is a little bit sweet, but when a memory is jogged, it surprises you, pushes you back with a thud, and you press your hands on top of your stomach to protect yourself when a hole opens up under your fingers, and a cold wind blows in, up under your ribs, aiming for your heart.

The longer her mother was gone, the more it was like a clock going backward. First, the slap of final moments, too raw to hold in your head for very long, and then the plaintive days leading up to the end, mixture of hope and comfort and continual drying from the medicines, as though all moisture, all water was being drained out of the room, out of her eyes, out of her body until there was nothing but bone and skin. When exactly did she go? It's such a gradual slide, talking to her one day, repeating for her the next, pushing her to talk, saying her name a little louder each day to keep her here as she sailed deeper and deeper into the ocean of her soul.

And then, in Stella's memory, she was younger, joking with doctors, visiting the sick, eating ice cream. Making fun with the plumber, the postman, the neighbor, the bus driver. And then younger still, yelling at Stella, crying from hurt, walking to town, brushing her hair. There were all the first firsts, and sometimes the second firsts: birthdays, Mother's Days, spring, favorite flowers, when they went here together, when they went there. It was the last thing that held Stella in place, in any place at all.

She often looked at people on the subways, all those people with ponytails, from little girls to grown men, all those bald people, small people, whole and broken people, the drunks, the preachers, the suits, and thought they were all babies, soft and tender. They were all somebody's baby once, and every one of them, except the very unlucky, loses their mother and their father. Child, you have a long road and a lonesome one with me gone. That was something big in common, like the inevitability of ants. It did not cheer her up.

People were alone the whole world over, and maybe, Stella thought, that makes us more alike than not. If only she could bridge the gap between her world and theirs. Everybody thinks their story is different, and it is. If we could all have half an hour to tell our stories, we would. Or would we? To the person in the shop, to the guy across the hall, to the woman standing next to you at the subway.

If Stella could tell her own story, she would.

SEVEN

Roots

Yep, I'm called Stella Dakota. Stella, named after a movie character and the stars.

Back in the Midwest, I was just Stella, and everybody else was just everybody else. But here, they always ask me what I am. Are you Mexican? You Polish? Stella, you have got to be Italian. And to be truthful, I couldn't say. My name is not much of anything, as far as I know. We ate spaghetti growing up, but we never called it pasta. St Patrick's Day was another day for Dad to drink a beer, maybe a few more, with his buddies, but nobody I knew put on green clothes. I'm pretty sure we're not Jewish; Ma used to cross herself whenever we drove by a church. Christmas was mostly about the turkey and once in a while a really good present like a baton or a baseball glove.

Dad used to call us "Heinz 57," same way they called mixed breeds of dogs, and he was kind of proud of it. I remember mom's mother making something she called "Real German Strudel," but it was just dry cake to us. And whenever Dad talked on the phone to his cousin in Topeka he would tell him to "stay away from firewater, Kemo Sabe." I never took much notice.

Here, everybody's from someplace else. I like that, but I don't always get where. It makes me feel a little like an alien, like I'm missing some big clue everybody else got. I think some of the guys in the market stare too much, but then I'm always looking at them, trying to work out where they are from. I thought somebody said Morocco, and somebody else said Lebanon, but we are all Americans, and it doesn't make much never mind.

Mrs W is nervous, but I started night school a couple of weeks ago. She says she worries because of all those late nights on the subway, but I think she worries I'll fail. Or worse, I won't fail and will move out of the neighborhood. Thing is, the thought of a new neighborhood is something I can't even bear. Imagine that; it was like another country or the moon when I first moved in, and now I expect I'd miss it.

In class, we all had to say something about ourselves. "Ice breaking," they called it, even though it was about a hundred degrees hot outside. Nobody would go first, so the teacher started a game. He put numbers in a desk drawer, and everybody had to take one. Then, he shouted out one number at a time, and if you had the number, you had to say a word that described yourself. One word. Hometown was important. Or a sports team you liked. Or favorite color. And the next time your number was called, you had to say something else, totally different from the first thing. Filling in the whole picture, one word at a time, the instructor said. I guess eleven is an unpopular number, because it took him forever to say it. When it finally came around to me, I was completely worked up about my favorite color (blue and orange are neck and neck, in my view) and beside myself trying to decide on a hometown.

So I hollered out Kansas, and everybody called me Dorothy from then on. I have learned to say Lawrence when asked and not mention Kansas (which is true) instead of Massachusetts (which is not). I worked it out that if you just said something that didn't sound weird like Brunei or Alaska, people were satisfied that they had your number and just moved on. They wanted to know you were from someplace, and that was good enough. Mostly, people leave me alone about it anymore.

Been almost five years here, two and a

half since I finished high school and left Aunt Wilma's. She was decent enough to have me live with her after Ma passed. Got me through school, and she was nice enough, I guess. She had her own way of doing things, and I got in her way lots of times. She called about every night when I first got the apartment, but she's down to once in a blue moon now.

It was strange coming here for a lot of reasons. Like anything else, I guess, some is good and some of it is not. Take the food. All that delicious soft food you eat with flatbread is from the Mid-east, but I never had it before I came here. And the pizza? A whole lot better, and they let you buy it in slices, which would never happen at Happy Joe's back home. A girl in night class introduced me to Vietnamese sandwiches from Chinatown, just about as cheap as they are good, and you can take them up to the Common and watch men dressed up like Ben Franklin getting ten bucks for having their picture taken by tourists from California. The sauce was like nothing I have ever tasted, and I liked it at once. But nobody warned me about the God Almighty hot peppers. I learned that one the hard way.

We talked about food in class, and that old feeling that I just do not, let me be clear, do not fit in here came down on me like a ton of bricks. My favorite meal? Bullheads, baby catfish, I said. I looked out at a room full of people staring at me like I had a melon on my head. We used to gut them on the sidewalk, too messy inside, and then flour them up and fry them in a pan. They were little, and you had to hold them in your hands like an ear of corn, careful not to swallow bones. Crispy and hot and delicious, there was nothing at all in the world like those little fish, if you didn't choke to death. When you added in potato salad and iced tea, it was heaven. And in the late summer, slices of tomatoes. Tomatoes are like gold here, and they taste something like Kleenex, with a soft scrape on your teeth and the flavor of air.

Places are places, and everybody has to be from somewhere. Everybody starts out strange, but there is nothing worse or better about where anybody comes from, in my view. I look at the Hmong guy in the supermarket comparing a can of shaving cream to a can of whipped cream. They look the same to him, and I hope he's not making pie. I watch the ladies with their scarves covering their bodies and much of their faces trying on bright red underwear at Marshalls, and I wonder what their life is like in their private worlds. I see old Chinese ladies, old as dust on dirt, fishing cans out of bins for the return money and wonder if anybody is looking out for them.

I have it on good authority that I now live in Red Sox Nation, which brings me to another set of questions about Big Green Monsters and dirty water. Being a fan made you an instant member of a group, and everybody is a fan when the team is winning. Some even when they are not.

In the park there are men asking for handouts, what my dad used to call "hobos." Which ones do I give money to and which ones do I pass by? Every one of them looks just as sad, like the world up and forgot them. Seven cents worth of God help us, Ma used to say. I could tell you everything there is to know about creek-walking or quarry-diving, but sharing the sidewalks with all these folks has me flat-out confused. If someone had a book of rules, it would help, but I think we're pretty much on our own, and unless you have a lick of sense, it's hard to figure.

So I wonder sometimes, in a world as big and weird as this one, just where do I fit in?

EIGHT

Found

She saw him at Park Street, standing on the middle platform with tracks on both sides where trains go in opposite directions. Some red-sneakered youngsters with electric speakers were warming up for the evening travelers' entertainment.

On top of his snow white hair sat a beret, a black beret, and he wore a dark duffle coat, the kind with toggles for buttons. He was small, with darting eyes and a fierce watchfulness. Shifting from one side to the other, he was searching for someone to answer his question. Stella saw him approach many people and watched as they moved away from him, one by one. She wondered just what he was looking for.

"This is to Cen-trál?"

"Pardon?"

Shrug.

"Cen-trál?"

Then, there was much pointing at the map on the wall covered with graffiti and gum, and too much detail about Maria's love life.

A couple of kids, college kids most likely, poked at him and turned him around, mimicking "Cen-trál, Cen-trál!"

And then he was in front of Stella. He popped up like a jack-in-the box and looked directly into Stella's eyes.

"Cen-trál?"

"Do you want to go to Central Square?"

"Most important!" he roared as he pointed at his watch and tore a piece of paper from his pocket. An audience with the governor, Stella thought. Maybe he was advising the mayor. Not likely.

Then Beret Man stabbed his finger at a circle on the map and pointed down the track, first in one direction and then the other. He lifted his shoulders as high as his curved ears and threw his arms out wide.

"Cen-trál!"

Stella nodded and began to count the stops for him on her fingers when the train rolled in, drowning out her words. When it stopped, she hesitated, then offered the open door.

"Okay, mister. Get on this train with me. I'll tell you when to get off."

No movement. Threads of people wove around the two of them, aiming for the opening.

"Come on!" She said, "Go Centrál!"

The old man swept his arm from his waist, out to the subway door, as though pulling back a magnificent curtain, and ushered his benefactress in.

They sat across from one another, his hand on his knees, his back as straight as a poker. He sent out the message that to come within a body's width would summon guards, dogs at the very least.

"In my country, astrophysicist, in this country, important meeting in Centrál Square!"

"Sure, sure. Well, it's just a couple of stops."

"Verrrry important. I become American. Verrrry soon."

The stop at Mass General brought many more people onto the T. Stella waited until the train was moving again for his monologue to start up, too.

"Most important scientist in my home. Degrees? Twenty. Teach in many universities. People pay to listen to me. Money!"

Are these the kind you have to worry about? thought Stella. Guys who go ballistic on public transportation and, I don't know, start attacking people? He doesn't seem the type, but he's sure worked up.

"Here, no work. Translate, fill in papers, BAHHH."

In fits and starts, Citizen Beret punched out details at the top of his voice. He sounded like he was giving orders, but he was really informing the crowd inside the car of his urgency. Their total and complete attention was required, as though the riders, through sheer concentration could move the subway that much faster. Naturally, everybody ignored him.

Well, they pretended to pay him no heed, but this was entertainment, too. As long as you didn't stare, Stella remembered. But, of course, she was locked in eye contact. She was his guide, his student, his witness on a train full of people shuttling up and over the bridge that stretched across the river.

"Attention passengers. We will be stopped here for traffic ahead. We're sorry for any inconvenience. Attention passengers. We will be stopped here for traffic ahead."

Mr Science was standing, walking, hands and arms in constant motion. As he warmed up, he began talking about his history, his past. He painted a picture with his short, loud sentences of triumphs and struggles and being an old man in a new world. By the time he got to his coming to America, Stella was surprised to catch heads bobbing, up and down the car.

There was no sign of moving that

subway, and the light spread out over the river, a little pink here, lapis blue above. Shoulders relaxed. People were listening. People were thinking.

"In Africa, I was a doctor. Here, seven years it will take to receive a license. Who has the money? I bathe people in a nursing home. Nice people. Old people."

"Tele-Vision sets. I fix tele-Vision sets. I can build bridges, dams. I fix tele-Vision sets now."

A sheep farmer worked in a shop, selling mobile phones. He had a special running. Anybody interested?

From different parts of the car, a few voices told what is lost by leaving the old country. And what is found. Getting his papers organized for citizenship, a famous man had to prove he wouldn't blow anything up. Or get on welfare. Or a hundred other things that people had to prove to come here and be American. Things Stella didn't ever think about.

"You born here?"

"No, not here."

"In America?"

"Well, yes, but another part, pretty far away."

Silence.

"You parents born here?"

"Yes, yes they were, but they are gone."

He bowed his head and clicked his mouth in sympathy. And she was a little proud that he was talking directly to her while the passengers watched without watching.

"You grrrrandparents born here?"

She liked the way his *r*'s took an age to come out, to get across the car to her.

"Far as I know."

"Well," he proclaimed. "You a rrrrrrrreal Yankee Doodle!" And he beamed, as though he had discovered, like an explorer on his own, without benefit of map or direction, nothing but good instincts and good fortune, a gem in the promised land hidden on the streets paved with gold, an Honest-to-God Real Article.

The car erupted in laughter that spread from one end to the other. Somebody whistled. The people sitting next to Stella patted her on the arm. One grandmother, with no sign of teeth in her head, broadly smiled and wiped her eyes, wet with mirth.

With a chug, the train jerked forward and in a few moments moved across the crest of the bridge and into the tunnel. One stop, two stops, and Stella extended her arms like a game show girl when the train came to a halt and opened its doors. Professor Cen-trál doffed his hat, took his triumph (did he bow, just a little?) and left the train.

People rode on. Some got off, some got on, and the merriment was diluted a little, but the car stayed warm, very warm, and eyes met and did not look away.

Stella rode on and on, and when the train came to its final station, she merged with the Lexington commuters, the backpacked students, the caretakers, the shop clerks and the fix-it men, the aspiring writers and the cleaning ladies crossing the highway to work. She felt the glint of Orion's belt, sent down from the steely sky, upon her American head and walked on.